Ding Dong

Written and illustrated by
An Vrombaut

Collins

Max is in his bat box.

2

It is Jill.

Max lets her in.

Jill has a big ring.

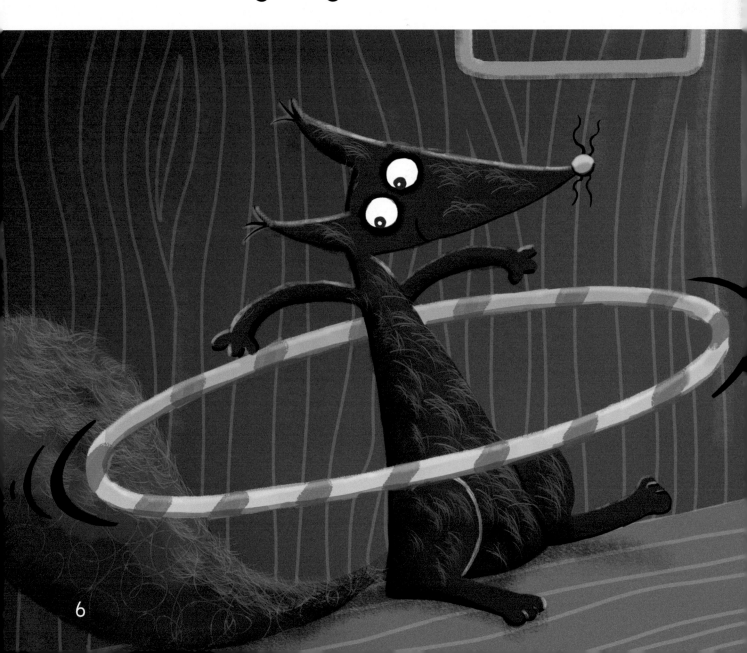

6

It is Jack.

He has dolls.

The bat box is full.

Max rings.

13

After reading

Letters and Sounds: Phase 3

Word count: 40

Focus phonemes: /ng/ /x/ /j/ zz

Common exception words: the, her, he, full

Curriculum links: Understanding the World: People and communities

Early learning goals: Reading: use phonic knowledge to decode regular words and read them aloud accurately, demonstrate understanding when talking with others about what they have read

Developing fluency

- Your child may enjoy hearing you read the book. Model fluency and expression.
- Encourage your child to have fun practising to read the words "ding dong" with expression as if a bell were ringing. Can you use different voices or tones?

Phonic practice

- Ask your child to sound talk and blend each of the following words: d/i/ng, s/i/ng, r/i/ng and w/i/ng.
- Ask your child:
  o Which of the following words contain the "ng" sound?
    Jack   sing   ping   fox   box   long   (*sing, ping, long*)
- Look at the "I spy sounds" on pages 14 to 15 together. Discuss the picture with your child. Can your child see any pictures of things that contain the /j/ and /x/ sounds? (*jam, jelly, juice, jug, Jack-in-a-box, jeep, taxi, fox, x-ray, Max*)

Extending vocabulary

- In the story, the bell makes the sound "ding dong". Ask your child:
  o What other words could we use to describe the noise of a bell? (e.g. *jingle, jangle, ting, ring, buzz, ding-a-ling, ping*)
- Explore other words that describe noises. Ask your child:
  o What noise does a drum make? (e.g. *boom, bang, thud*)
  o What noise does a horn make? (e.g. *beep, toot*)